The BEST Pirate

For everyone who's
ever felt a bit small
S.M.

For Sam, with love
D.T.

First published in 2016 by Scholastic Children's Books
Euston House, 24 Eversholt Street
London NW1 1DB
a division of Scholastic Ltd
www.scholastic.co.uk
London · New York · Toronto · Sydney · Auckland
Mexico City · New Delhi · Hong Kong

Text copyright © 2016 Sue Mongredien
Illustrations copyright © 2016 Dan Taylor

PB ISBN 978 1 4071 3614 1

The BEST Pirate

Sue Mongredien

Dan Taylor

SCHOLASTIC

Pirate Dave was big and brave,

Pirate Nell was clever,

Pirate Giles could swim for miles
In any kind of weather.

But **Pirate Paul**...well, he was small.
He was hardly a proper pirate at all.

(Or so the others thought...)

On Monday morning, day was dawning —
Dave raised the pirate flag.
"A treasure-hunting we shall go,
For gold and jewels and swag."

Nell checked the map while Giles looked out.
The sky was bright and blue.
Pirate Paul jumped up and down
And asked, "What shall *I* do?"

"I could swab the deck,

or patch the sails,

Or make the portholes shiny?

I could climb the rigging to watch for whales..."
But **Dave** scoffed, "You're too tiny."

Poor **Pirate Paul** was just so teeny.
There *was* no work for one so weeny.

(Or so the pirates thought...)

THE ELUSIVE GIANT SQUID
G.T. HILL

On they sailed through sun then hail
As **Nell** steered north-north-east.
Dave caught dabs and crayfish and crabs
For a midday pirate feast.

Down in the kitchen, **Giles** got mixing.
"I'll help!" **Paul** cried keenly.
"I could make sauce or wash up, of course."
But his shipmates sniggered meanly.

"You're just a baby, **Pirate Paul**.
And far too small to help at all."

(That's what those pirates thought...)

After a while, **Dave** gave a smile,
"Ah-hargh! There's land ahead!"
"Treasure's near!" the pirates cheered.
"We'll soon be rich!" **Nell** said.

Down went the anchor, up went the sails.
The ship slid into shore.
Armed with rope and a telescope
They set off to explore.

But **Pirate Paul** was just too teeny,
There was no use for one so weeny.

(Well, that's what the pirates *thought*...)

Nell checked her map. "X marks the spot.
This is the way to go.
Ten paces **north**, then twenty **east**,

And **then** we need to...

Back on ship, **Paul** patched the sails
And made the portholes shine.

After a while he scratched his head.
"They're taking a **very long time**."

Down in a pit, the others were stuck.
A spider made brave **Dave** yell.
Try as they might, they couldn't climb out.

"I hear something coming,"
hissed **Nell**.

Less-brave **Dave** shivered.

Nell quaked and quivered.

And **Giles** whimpered,
"I want my mummy!"

Out on the ship, **Paul** heard the great roar
And then the poor pirates' scared calls.

"Fear not!" he cried as he leapt to his feet.
"Because here comes...

Cannonball Paul shot onto the scene.
The tiger galloped away.

The pirates cheered as **Paul** hauled them out.
And everyone shouted,

"HOORAY!"

"Thank you, oh thank you," sighed **Dave**, **Giles** and **Nell**.

Then **Paul** pointed, "X marks the spot!"

They dug up the gold and the sparkling jewels.
There really were rather a lot.

Later that evening, back on the ship,
As the sun slowly sank in the west,
Everyone cheered for their new captain: **Paul**!

The smallest, the bravest, the **best**!

TREASURE MAP

MERMAID CAVES

GIANT GRUMPY SQUID

SCARY QUICKSAND

JUNGLE

MAN-EATING PLANTS

SWAMP

UNEXPECTED PIT

JAGGED CLIFFS

SHARKS